___ONCE-UPON-A-TIME TALES___
BEAUTY & THE BEAST

NEW SEASONS

PUBLISHING

Copyright © 1992 Publications International, Ltd.
ISBN 1-56173-496-9
Adapted by Jane Jerrard
Illustrations by Burgandy Nilles

There once was a rich man who had six children—three daughters and three sons. After a lifetime of good luck, the man suddenly fell upon hard times. His house burned down, his ships sank at sea, and his business partner ran off with all his money.

He and his children were forced to move into a small cottage in the country, where they lived on food they raised themselves. His two oldest daughters were very unhappy with this change, but the youngest, named Beauty, tried to make their new life as comfortable as possible.

One day the man heard that one of his ships had sailed safely into harbor. He decided to go there to see this for himself, though it was a long ride.

His children all asked their father to bring back expensive presents. But Beauty asked only for her father's safe return.

"Isn't there anything I can bring you, Beauty?" asked her father.

"If you see one, I would like to have a rose," said Beauty, for she missed the beautiful gardens around their old home.

Beauty's father reached the town safely, only to find that his ship had been robbed, and he was now poorer than before. Making his way back home through a thick forest, the unlucky man was lost in a terrible snowstorm.

Suddenly, up ahead, he saw a row of flowering trees and at the same time felt warm air on his face!

The man had discovered an enchanted castle. He explored the gardens—where no snow had fallen—then went inside, though no one would answer the door.

He found a cheerful little room with a table of fresh food waiting for him. He ate hungrily, then fell asleep in front of the fire.

The next morning, there was still no sign of anyone, so the man got ready to leave. On his way through the gardens, he picked a rose for Beauty. Suddenly, an ugly Beast appeared, as if by magic! "So this is how you thank me? I feed and shelter you and then you steal from me?" said the Beast.

The man begged for his life, explaining that the rose was for one of his daughters.

The Beast said that he would not kill the man but would accept one of his daughters instead. He promised to treat her kindly if she would come to live with him.

The man returned home and told his children what had happened. All six agreed that since Beauty's rose had started the trouble, she must be the one to go. The very next, day she rode away bravely with her father.

Again, they found no one in the castle, and again, supper was set on the table. But this time, the Beast appeared as they finished eating. Beauty was very frightened by the Beast's terrible face, but he spoke to her gently, asking if she would stay with him in order to save her father's life.

Beauty told the Beast that she would stay. So her father left her there (though it broke his heart), and she made the Beast's castle her home. She had her own big room with mirrors for walls and a clock that woke her by calling her name. She spent her days alone, exploring the wonders of the enchanted castle, and ate dinner each evening with the Beast. Soon, she was no longer afraid of him.

"Am I very ugly?" he asked her each night. She would answer that he was, but that she liked him anyway.

"Then will you marry me, Beauty?" he would say, and she would beg him not to ask her that question.

Beauty was happy in the magical castle, and she had grown very fond of the Beast. But she never stopped missing her own home and her brothers and sisters and her loving father.

One night at dinner she asked the Beast to let her go home for a visit. He made her promise to come back in two months and gave her two magical trunks to fill with presents for her family. No matter how much she packed, the trunks were never full.

Then he gave her a ring with a large jewel in it and told her it would take her home and bring her back. All she had to do was turn it on her finger, and she would be home the next day!

The next morning, Beauty awoke to the sound of her father's voice! She was home, in her own bed. Her family was very happy to see her. Her father's luck had finally returned, and they were rich once more.

As the weeks passed, Beauty missed the castle where she had been so happy. Mostly she missed the Beast and the way they would talk each night. But she was afraid to tell her family she wanted to leave.

One night she put the magic ring on her finger and looked into the jewel. There she saw the Beast, lying in his garden. He seemed to be dying! Beauty turned the ring on her finger and was suddenly by his side.

"Oh, please don't die, gentle Beast!" cried Beauty. "I never knew it before, but I love you!"

At Beauty's words, there was a sudden flash of light, and the Beast leaped up. Beauty saw that her ugly friend had changed into a handsome prince! Beauty's love had freed the prince from a terrible spell. Since the two already loved each other, they married and lived happily ever after in the enchanted castle.